The Big White Box

First published in 2012
by Wayland

Text copyright © Tom Easton 2012
Illustration copyright © Woody Fox 2012

Wayland
338 Euston Road
London NW1 3BH

Wayland Australia
Level 17/207 Kent Street
Sydney, NSW 2000

Series Editor: Louise John
Series design: D. R. ink
Design: Lisa Peacock
Consultant: Shirley Bickler

A CIP catalogue record for this book is available from the British Library.

ISBN 9780750268615

Printed in China

Wayland is a division of Hachette Children's Books,
an Hachette UK company
www.hachette.co.uk

The Big White Box

Written by Tom Easton
Illustrated by Woody Fox

WAYLAND

It was late and Sea Force Four were ready for bed. Polly Porpoise liked to sleep in the seaweed.

Blob Pufferfish slept on the coral and Zip Marlin slept on the move!

Luna Lampfish slept in a hollow in the rocks, but she wasn't happy.

It was too small, and the other fish kept coming over to use her lamp. It kept her awake.

"If only I had my own little place," she said.

Suddenly the clam phone bubbled.
Zip got there first. "Sea Force Four!"
he said. "How can we help?"

"Come, quick!" a turtle croaked.
"We've found a funny box on the
seabed and my boy is trapped in it!"

Sea Force Four whizzed off.
Zip lead the way.

When they arrived, Mama and
Papa Turtle were very worried.

Sea Force Four looked at the big white box. Luna shone her light so they could get a better look.

"Junior is stuck inside!" Papa said.
"Don't worry," Luna replied. "Blob
is very strong. He'll open it."

"The box is called a fridge," said clever Polly. "It keeps food cold."

Blob wrapped his tail around the handle and pulled hard, but the fridge did not open.

"Oh dear," Mama Turtle moaned,
flapping her flippers.

"Let me help," Zip said.

"We'll pull, too," said the others.
Sea Force Four pulled and pulled.
At last, the door popped open and
Junior swam out!

"This fridge thing is dangerous,"
Blob said. "We need to find a way
to recycle it."

"Cycle it?" asked Zip. "But it doesn't have wheels."

"Not cycle," Polly laughed. "Recycle. It means to use something again."

"Look!" shouted Luna, suddenly, flashing her light.

A big, toothy shark was heading towards them, looking hungry!

"Hurry!" shouted Polly. "Get into the fridge!"

"Don't close the door," Blob shouted.
"We won't be able to get out!"

There was a big crash as the shark knocked the fridge over. His jaws crunched and he ripped the door off!

Sea Force Four were very worried.
The shark spat out the door and
came towards them.

"Don't worry everyone. I'll take care of this!" said Zip, and he shot off.

The shark zoomed after him.
The others hid until it was safe and then they climbed out of the fridge.

"Oh no," Blob said. "We'll never see him again!"

"See who?" asked Zip from behind them. Everyone jumped.

"How did you get there?" Luna asked, shining her light in his face.

"I used my super speed to lead him away," laughed Zip, "and here I am!"

"We still need to recycle the fridge," Polly said.

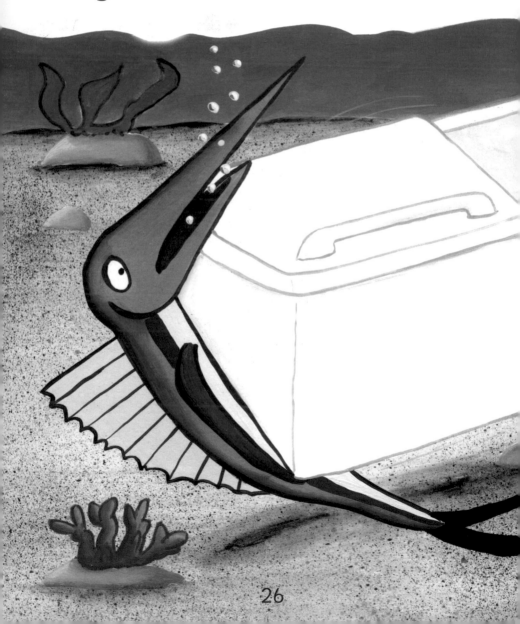

"We'll take it back to base. I have an idea!" Luna said.

Back at base, Sea Force Four put
the fridge down.

"The shark broke the door," Luna said, "so I won't be trapped. I have a nice place to sleep at last!"

Luna swam inside the fridge.
"Perfect," she called, happily.

"Won't she be cold in there?"
Zip asked.

"Oh, Zip," said Blob, rolling his eyes.
"I'll tell you later!"

START READING is a series of highly enjoyable books for beginner readers. The books have been carefully graded to match the Book Bands widely used in schools. This enables readers to be sure they choose books that match their own reading ability.

Look out for the Band colour on the book in our Start Reading logo.

The Bands are:

Pink Band 1

Red Band 2

Yellow Band 3

Blue Band 4

Green Band 5

Orange Band 6

Turquoise Band 7

Purple Band 8

Gold Band 9

START READING books can be read independently or shared with an adult. They promote the enjoyment of reading through satisfying stories supported by fun illustrations.

Tom Easton is an experienced author of children's books, including lots of funny Start Reading books about the Poor Pirates! He lives with his family in Surrey.

Woody Fox has been illustrating children's books for 18 years! He was born in London, but now lives in a cute thatched cottage in the middle of Devon with his 2 cats. When he's not drawing, he likes to do mosaics, basket weaving and go for long walks!